Where Wild Horses Run

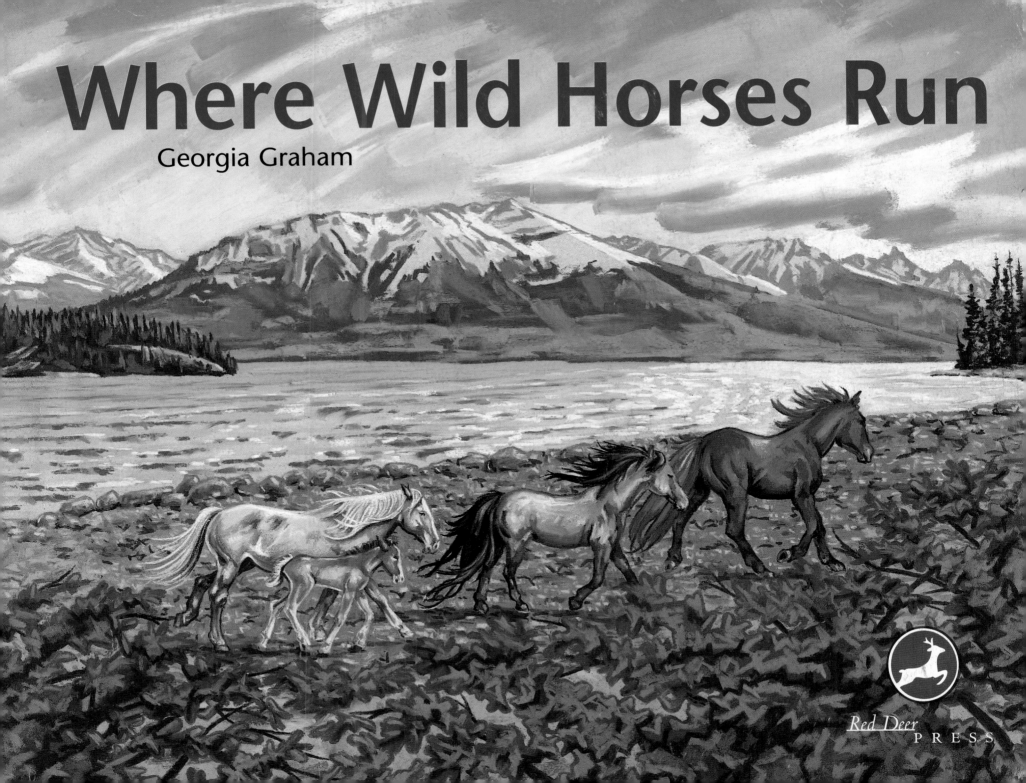

Where Wild Horses Run

Georgia Graham

Red Deer PRESS

^Steam rises from Brown Foal's wet coat. Snowflakes vanish as they float onto her newborn shaking body. She is bewildered by the cold. Mother's tongue kneads warmth down to her bones.

After only one hour Brown Foal arches her back and struggles to her wobbling legs. She scrambles to keep up as the band starts to travel down the valley looking for food.

The last spring snow has disappeared by midday. Brown Foal nurses from her patient mother while the band devours sweet blades of new grass.

Before long, Brown Foal learns to leap and play with Gray Colt. Soon she can race circles around him.

The horses wander through a forest toward the meadow on the other side. Low down on a tree trunk are deep scratches from Black Bear. But higher on the trunk loom immense gashes that are not from Black Bear.

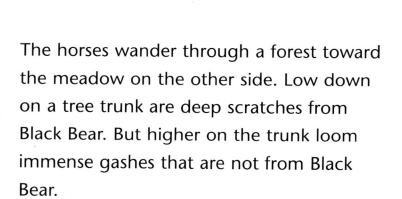

Brown Foal's mother prances with uneven steps. Brown Foal becomes anxious. The horses are nervous because of the scent that lingers on the tree bark.

They know they are moving through Grizzly Bear's forest.

A heavy presence hangs in the air. A twig snaps not far from Brown Foal. She spots a flash of white teeth through the branches. Whinnying, she kicks up her hind legs.

Gold Stallion snorts and stomps quickly and heavily. Wild-eyed, the horses begin to trot and then to gallop.

A hungry grizzly is stalking them through the trees. He is thin from his winter slumber, and his eyes are fixed on Brown Foal. Mother nudges Brown Foal to the center of the band.

The band is bolting in fear now. Swerving trees and leaping boulders, Brown Foal is as sure footed and swift as the rest of the horses. Grizzly bounds along beside them. Brown Foal keeps up as they burst onto a meadow and tear across the open ground.

Finally, Grizzly gives up the chase. He turns and lumbers back into his forest, exhausted and still hungry.

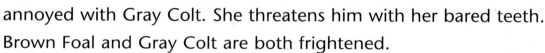

The meadows are covered with tender green shoots. The band grazes on the valley's sloping shoulders, warm sun on their backs.

Now that Grizzly is gone, Brown Foal plays with Gray Colt again, running and springing and chasing. But Lead Mare is annoyed with Gray Colt. She threatens him with her bared teeth. Brown Foal and Gray Colt are both frightened.

Gray Colt is over two winters old, almost full grown, but there is only room in the band for one stallion. Gold Stallion charges Gray Colt to banish him forever. Gray Colt flees to the edge of the meadow, turns and looks back at the band. Gold Stallion stomps a warning, and Gray Colt disappears into the forest.

Brown Foal strains to catch a final glimpse of her friend. Will she ever see him again?

Every day the horses wander the meadows, grazing. Then Brown Foal spots movement in the forest. Has Gray Colt returned? Brown Foal prances excitedly. The mares stop grazing. Gold Stallion's ears stand tall. Suddenly, several unknown mares and a foal appear out of the trees.

Brown Foal whinnies an alert, and Gold Stallion turns around as an enormous roan stallion thunders forward, powerful muscles rippling, his coat shining like the rising sun. He is older and stronger than Gold Stallion. He circles, stomping and grunting in low fast breaths. He paws the earth.

Brown Foal narrowly escapes Roan Stallion's path as he charges at Gold Stallion. Smaller, but as fast as an

arrow, Gold Stallion slashes Roan Stallion's shoulder with his front hoof. Roan is dazed by the fresh wound.

As fast as they appeared, Roan and his band retreat in a storm of dust. Gray Colt isn't part of Roan's band. Gold Stallion steers his band up the valley to widen their distance from Roan Stallion.

The lower meadows are draped in a blanket of green. The band is being spied on from a hilltop by a herd of curious bachelor horses. Brown Foal sees a gray coat. Is that Gray Colt? She runs ahead to look closer. She sees that one horse is gray but he's an old stallion.

Gold Stallion stomps and grumbles a warning to stay back. The bachelors disappear behind the horizon. All but one — Old Gray Stallion. The mares stop grazing and look up at him intently. They know him well. He was their stallion before Gold defeated him in their final battle, long before Brown Foal's time. Gold paces wildly now. Old Gray Stallion slowly ambles away, his head hanging low.

Gold Stallion presses his mares toward the sound of the river's roar. He is heading for the pastures beyond, pastures far away from Old Gray Stallion and Roan Stallion.

The band travels along the bank searching for a welcoming spot to cross. Brown Foal has never seen or heard a rushing river before. She shudders, fearful of the roaring fury.

The river wells up in deep calm pools. Beavers have built a dam with tightly tangled sticks and branches. Then the river trickles into a narrow stream.

Gold Stallion and Lead Mare start to move carefully along the pile of tangled branches. The river bed is also blanketed with scattered sticks. All the horses follow, Brown Foal close to her mother. As she steps into the river, Brown Foal's tiny hoof becomes trapped in the mesh of twigs. She panics, flailing wildly. She twists her leg, trying to free herself. Her leg throbs with pain. She is limping badly.

The horses in the lead climb up the river bank and quicken their pace. Mother nervously lags behind with Brown Foal as she presses through the water.

Hidden behind boulders, as still as a tree stump, Cougar is poised, ready to pounce. Brown Foal struggles onto the grassy bank and hobbles after her mother. Cougar springs forward.

As if from nowhere, Gray Colt appears like a bolt of lightning right in front of Cougar. Stunned, Cougar hesitates. Gray Colt's eyes are flashing with fury as he charges. Cougar is racing away.

Brown Foal limps after her mother. Her place is in Gold Stallion's band. But someday Gray Colt may be a powerful young stallion with his own band of mares. And Brown Foal may grow to be Brown Mare with a foal of her own . . . where wild horses run.

Published by Red Deer Press
A Fitzhenry & Whiteside Company
195 Allstate Parkway,
Markham, ON L3R 4T8
www.reddeerpress.com

Published in the United States by Red Deer Press
311 Washington Street
Brighton, Massachusetts 02135

Edited by Peter Carver
Cover and interior design by Blair Kerrigan
Printed and bound in Hong Kong, China by Sheck Wah Tong in June 2011, job 54397

Red Deer Press acknowledges with thanks the Canada Council for the Arts, and the Ontario Arts Council for their support of our publishing program. We acknowledge the financial support of the Government of Canada through the Canada Book Fund for our publishing activities.

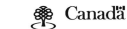 

THE CANADA COUNCIL | LE CONSEIL DES ARTS
FOR THE ARTS | DU CANADA
SINCE 1957 | DEPUIS 1957

Canadä

ONTARIO ARTS COUNCIL
CONSEIL DES ARTS DE L'ONTARIO

Library and Archives Canada Cataloguing in Publication
Graham, Georgia, 1959-
    Where wild horses run / written and illustrated by Georgia Graham.
ISBN 978-0-88995-448-9
    I. Title.
PS8563.R33W44 2011   jC813'.54   C2011-901431-9

Publisher Cataloging-in-Publication Data (U.S)
Graham, Georgia
    Where wild horses run / Georgia Graham.
[32] p. : col. ill. ; cm.
Summary: A moving story of how one band of horses grouped together as a family to protect a vulnerable colt from a cougar; a story of love and dedication that will ultimately inspire children with the hope that there are still truly wild places in the world worth our protection.
ISBN: 978-0-88995-448-9
1. Horses -- Juvenile fiction. I. Title.
[Fic] dc22   PZ7.G73436Wh   2011

Dedication
To the wild horses of the Nemaiah Valley, BC.
I went there to look for the horses in the middle of May when they were still low in the hills searching for the first blades of spring grass. There I found four bands, each led by a stallion rippling with muscles and jealously protecting his mares. There were very few foals because their predators are many. My hope is that humans will not be another threat but leave the wild horses to be magnificent and free.
— Georgia Graham